Oedipus and the Sphinx, Attic red drinking cup, circa 480-470 BC, Gregorian Etruscan Museum, Vatican Museums.

Scale: 1 inch equals 40 miles

0	20	40	60	MILES (ML) 100

0   50 KILOMETERS (KM) 100

Map by Myken Bomberger

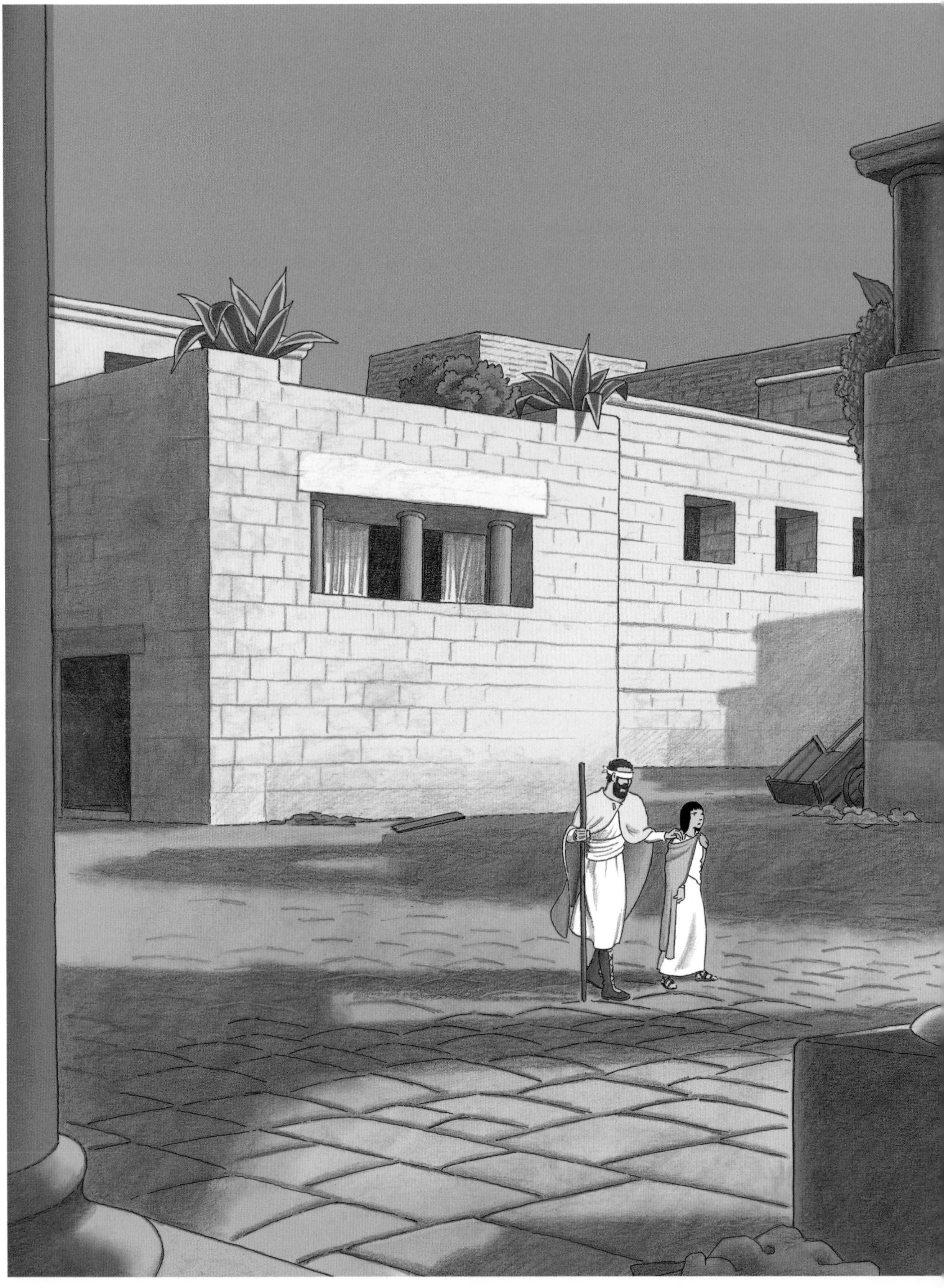

YVAN POMMAUX

OEDIPUS

TRAPPED BY DESTINY

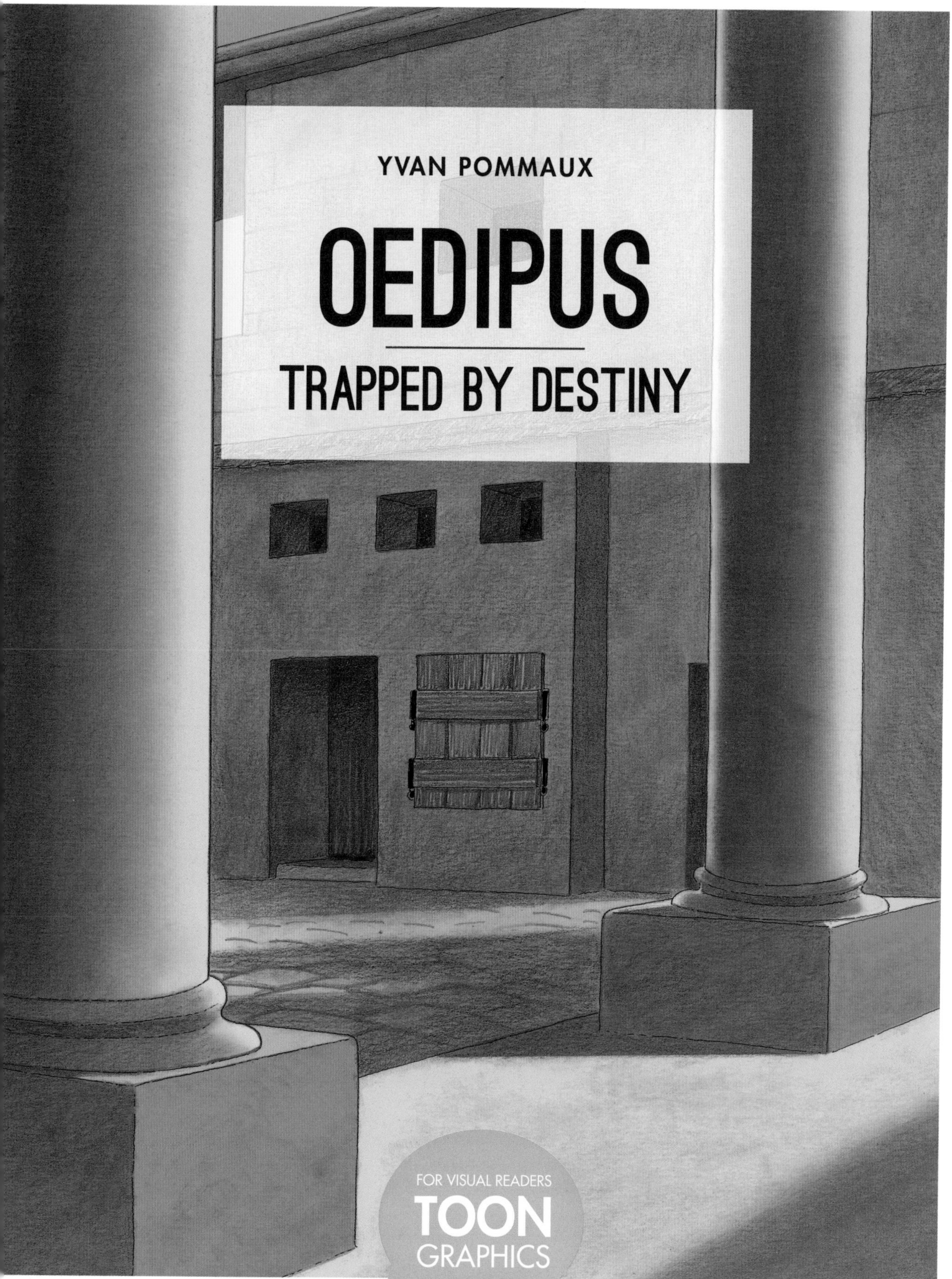

FOR VISUAL READERS
TOON
GRAPHICS

Editorial Direction & Book Design: FRANÇOISE MOULY

Editorial Consultant: DASH

Coloring: NICOLE POMMAUX

YVAN POMMAUX'S artwork was drawn in pencil and india ink and colored digitally.

A TOON Graphic™ © 2016 TOON Books, an imprint of RAW Junior, LLC, 27 Greene Street, New York, NY 10013. Original text and illustrations from *Oedipe l'enfant trouvé* © 2010 l'école des loisirs, Paris. Translation, ancillary material, and TOON Graphic™ adaptation © 2016 RAW Junior, LLC. No part of this book may be used or reproduced in any manner whatsoever without written permission except in the case of brief quotations embodied in critical articles and reviews. TOON Graphics™, TOON Books®, LITTLE LIT® and TOON Into Reading!™ are trademarks of RAW Junior, LLC. All rights reserved. All our books are Smyth Sewn (the highest library-quality binding available) and printed with soy-based inks on acid-free, woodfree paper harvested from responsible sources. Printed in China by C&C Offset Printing Co., Ltd. Distributed to the trade by Consortium Book Sales and Distribution, Inc.; orders (800) 283-3572; orderentry@perseusbooks.com; www.cbsd.com.

Library of Congress Cataloging-in-Publication Data:

Pommaux, Yvan, author, illustrator. [Oedipe. English] Oedipus: Trapped by Destiny / Yvan Pommaux; Translated by Richard Kutner. pages cm "A TOON Graphic." ISBN 978-1-935179-95-5 (hardcover : alk. paper) 1. Oedipus (Greek mythological figure)--Juvenile literature. 2. Oedipus (Greek mythological figure)--Comic books, strips, etc. 3. Graphic novels. I. Kutner, Richard, translator. II. Title. BL820.O43P6613 2015 741.5'944--dc23 2015029257

ISBN 978-1-935179-95-5 (hardcover)

16 17 18 19 20 21 C&C 10 9 8 7 6 5 4 3 2 1

WWW.TOON-BOOKS.COM

YVAN POMMAUX

OEDIPUS
TRAPPED BY DESTINY

Translated by RICHARD KUTNER

A TOON GRAPHIC

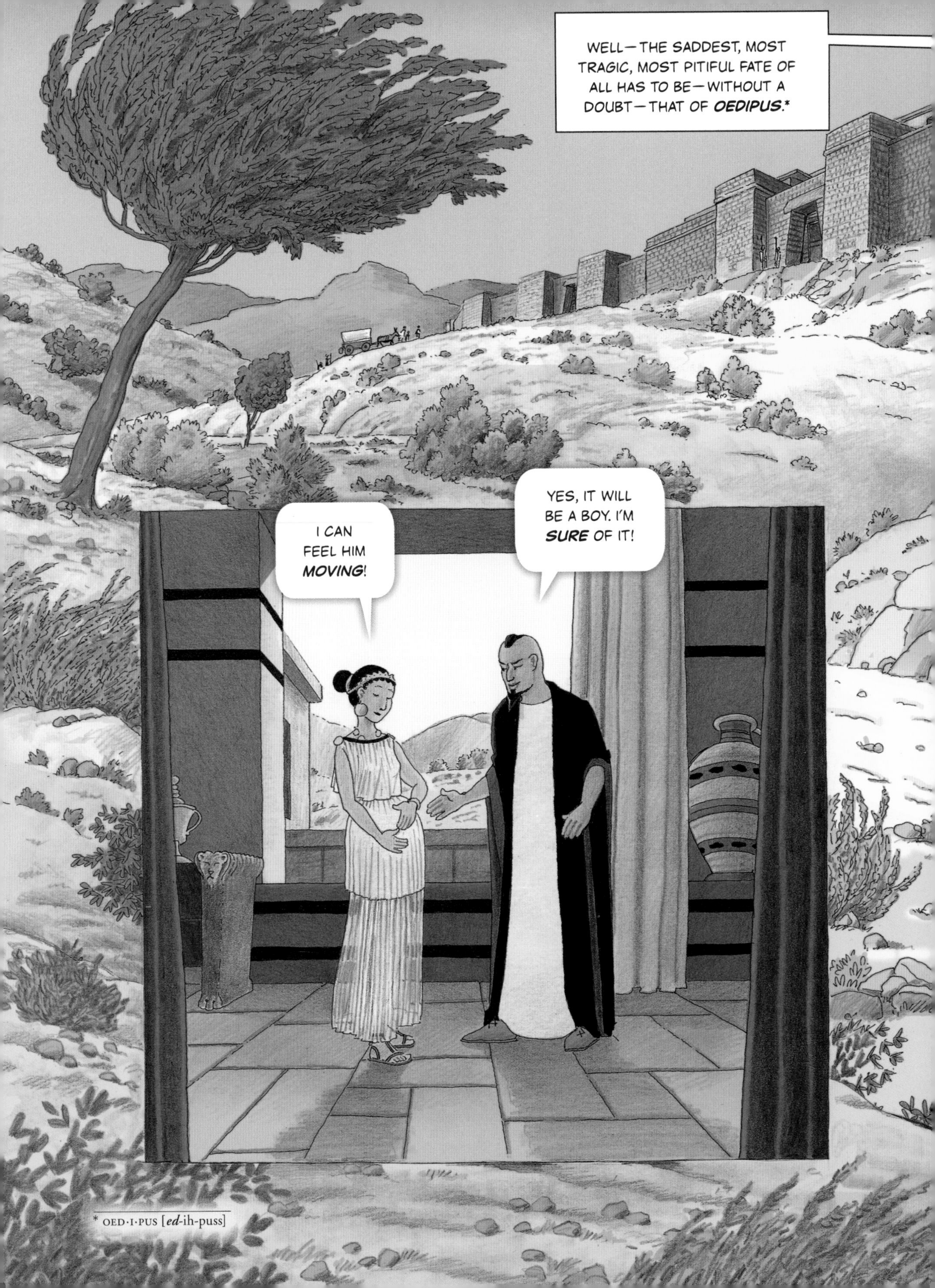
WELL—THE SADDEST, MOST TRAGIC, MOST PITIFUL FATE OF ALL HAS TO BE—WITHOUT A DOUBT—THAT OF ***OEDIPUS***.*
I CAN FEEL HIM ***MOVING***!
YES, IT WILL BE A BOY. I'M ***SURE*** OF IT!

* OED·I·PUS [*ed*-ih-puss]

HIS STORY STARTS BEFORE HE'S EVEN *BORN*...

King Laius* was overjoyed when his wife, Queen Jocasta,* told him she was pregnant. But there was one thing that troubled him. As the ruler of Thebes,* a magnificent military stronghold in the heart of ancient Greece, the king was eager for a male heir to his throne. Before the child was even born, he decided to travel to the Temple of Apollo* at Delphi.*

* LAI·US [*lay*-iss] / JO·CAS·TA [jo-*kass*-ta]
THEBES [*theebz*] / A·POL·LO [uh-*pahl*-oh]
DEL·PHI [*dell*-fie]

At the temple, pilgrims didn't see the god Apollo. Instead, they saw a woman in a trance, the Pythia,* an oracle* who gave answers from the gods in the form of chants and strange cries. Laius had come hoping to hear of his future son's many great exploits, but instead he was met with a terrible prediction...

Laius, like all Ancient Greeks, knew that the gods' prophecies always came true. He returned to Thebes devastated.

And so, when Jocasta gave birth to a baby boy, Laius was stricken with terror instead of joy.

...AND MAKE SURE HE **NEVER** COMES BACK!

Laius ordered his most faithful servant to take the child and abandon him at the top of Mount Cithaeron,* an arid and isolated mountain overlooking the Gulf of Corinth.*

WAAA

The servant tied the baby's feet to a stake, abandoning him to the wild beasts. Surely, no infant could survive that.

WAAAAAAH WAAA
WAAA

But, as fate would have it, a shepherd from Corinth named Phorbas* heard his frightened cries. Phorbas untied the infant, gave him some sheep's milk, and took him to the King and Queen of Corinth, Polybus* and Merope,* who were distraught not to have children of their own.

The royal couple gladly adopted the baby, whose feet were still marked by the ropes. They named him Oedipus, which means swollen feet. Oedipus happily grew up as a treasured prince in the royal palace of Corinth.

* PHOR·BAS [*for*-biss] / POL·Y·BUS [*pahl*-ee-biss]
MER·O·PE [*merr*-oh-pee]

As he got older, the handsome Oedipus became known as a proud and impulsive prince, whose privileged status incited jealousy. But the true nature of his birth couldn't remain a secret forever. One day, he overheard a rumor at the marketplace...

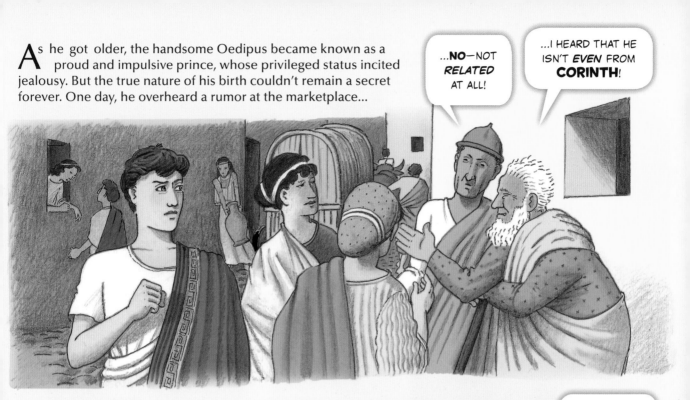

He ran to ask the king and queen about his birth. His parents, who had loved him and raised him as their own, had never told him the truth about how he had been found. Overwhelmed, they denied the rumor.

But doubt had been planted in Oedipus's mind. He saw only one way to know who he really was and what lay in store for him–he set out to ask the oracle of Delphi about his fate.

Unfortunately, Oedipus, like his father, was to find nothing but sorrow at the temple...

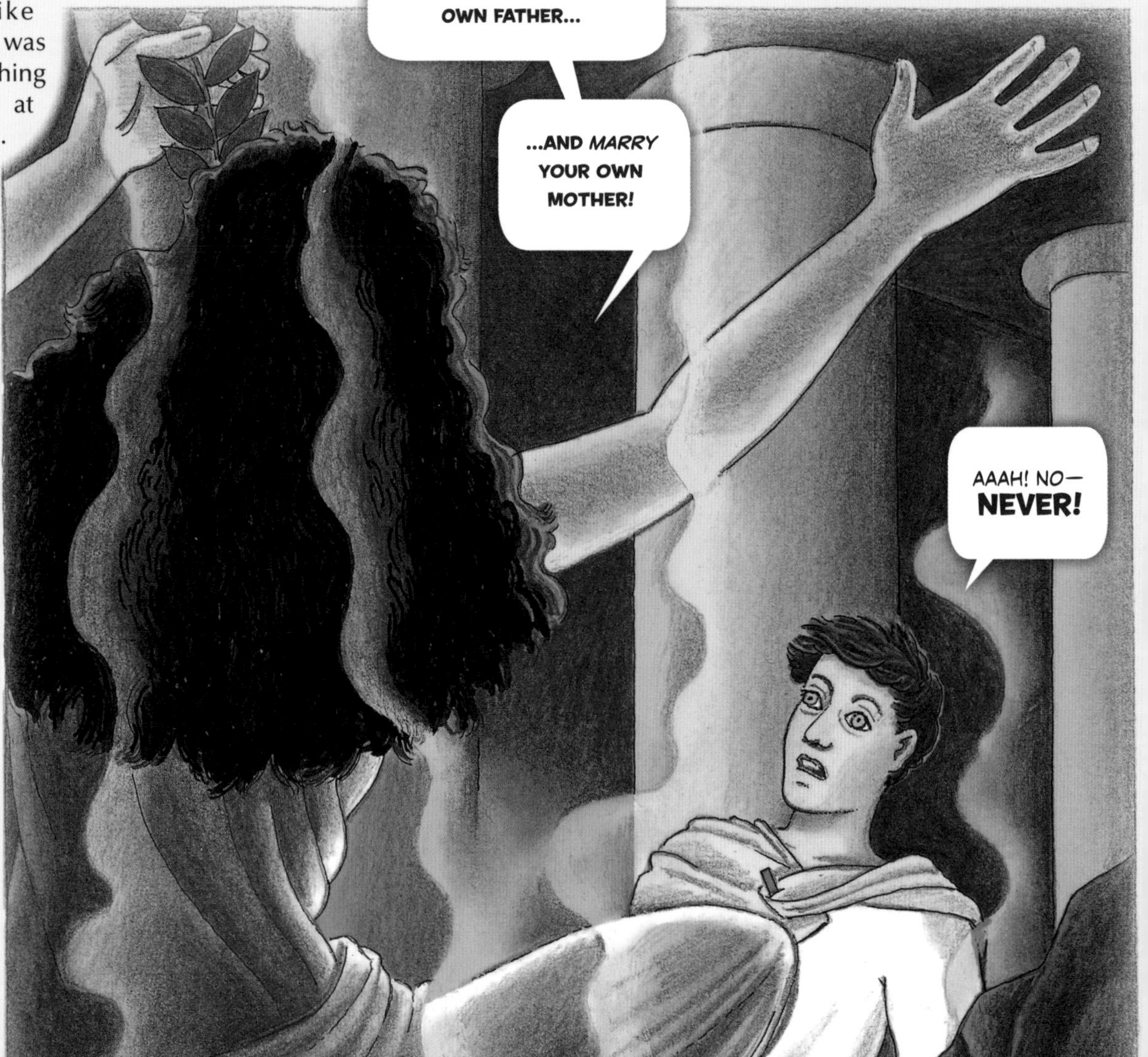
YOU WILL *KILL* YOUR OWN FATHER...
...AND *MARRY* YOUR OWN MOTHER!
AAAH! NO— NEVER!

The oracle's prophecy was truly horrifying for Oedipus. The young prince ran screaming from the temple.

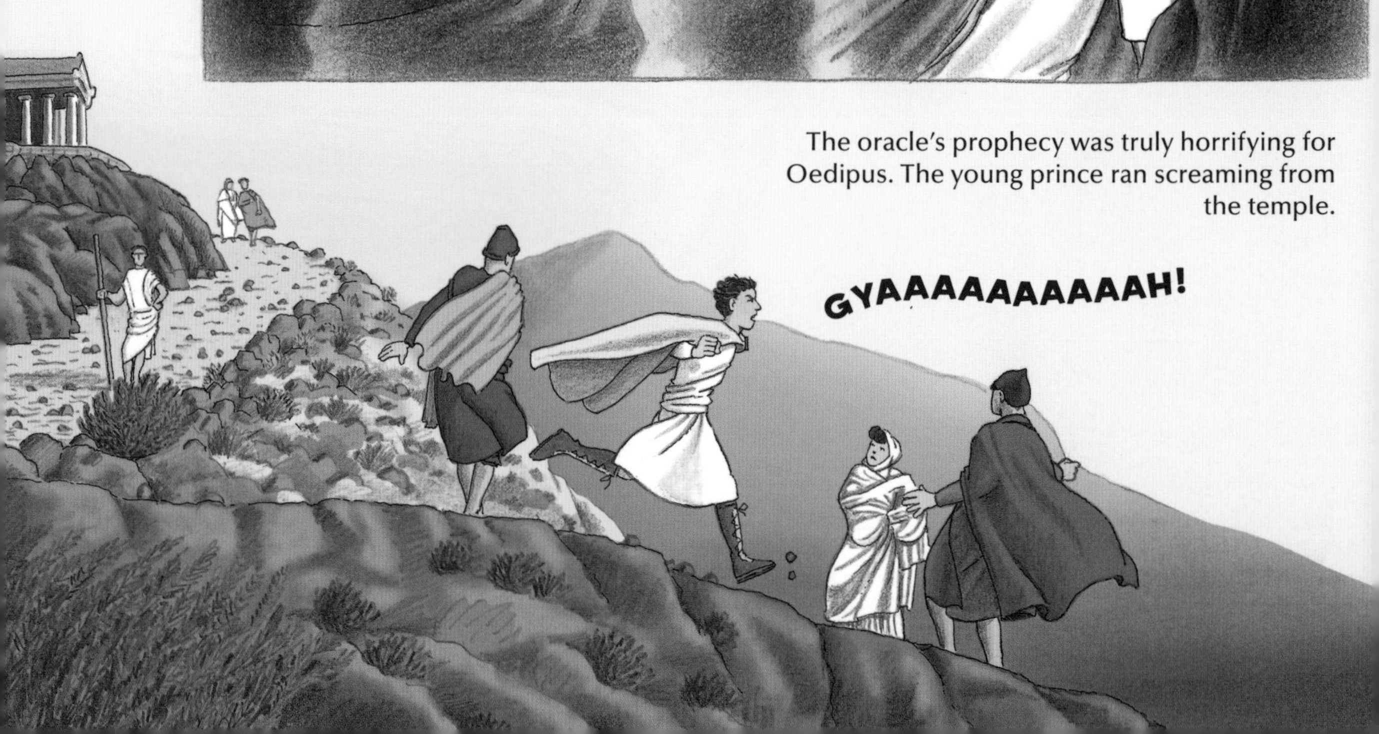
GYAAAAAAAAAAH!

Blinded by unbearable pain and anguish, Oedipus fled. He ran and ran—not knowing where he was going, wanting only to escape far from the oracle, far from his parents, far from what he'd been told was his fate. At some point in his wild journey, he found himself at a place where three roads met. A cart and its escorts blocked his path...

Still wild with anger and despair, the enraged Oedipus attacked the men who provoked him.

Though he was outnumbered, Oedipus was quick and powerful. He quickly dispatched most of the men, all but one falling to the young prince's sword.

In his fury, Oedipus overturned the cart. The old man in it was thrown from his seat, struck his head on a stone, and died immediately. As quickly as things had started, they were over. Oedipus, calming down, realized he was now a murderer. The image of the place where the three roads met would forever be engraved in his memory.

Oedipus began walking, but not back to Corinth. He had no more doubts: he was certain he was the son of Polybus and Merope, since the Pythia hadn't mentioned the rumor to the contrary. He saw only one way to ward off the terrible curse threatening his parents: stay far away from the city where he had grown up and never return.

Over time, Oedipus regained his composure. He made a
decision that put his mind at ease: he would never again lose
control of himself or give in to violence. Wherever he went, he
would help people and try to resolve conflicts.

His travels led him to Boeotia,* where he learned that Thebes, the formidable capital, was under a state of siege. The Sphinx,* a winged monster with a woman's head and a lion's body, was blocking access to the city. It jumped in front of any traveler who approached Thebes and asked him a riddle, which he had to solve or else be devoured.

No one had solved the riddle, and the city was cut off from the rest of the world. There was almost no food left.

I KNOW WHAT I MUST DO...THE PEOPLE OF THEBES WILL NO LONGER LIVE IN TERROR!

THIS PLACE SEEMS SO FAMILIAR... BUT NO—I MUST JUST KNOW IT FROM THE STORYTELLERS' DESCRIPTIONS....

As he climbed Mount Cithaeron, Oedipus felt a strange sensation: was it possible that he knew this spot? He was lost in thought when suddenly, in the sound of the wind, he heard the beating of wings.

There, at the edge of a precipice, crouched the sphinx, flapping her powerful wings of gold and bronze. She extended her beautiful face almost lovingly—but her eyes gleamed with a spark of cruelty. Her lion's body curled up and undulated, and her tail lashed at the ground.

MANY TRAVELERS HAVE COME THROUGH HERE, AND HERE MOST HAVE **FALLEN**.
ANSWER MY ***RIDDLE*** OR YOU WILL JOIN *THEM*.

Oedipus thought hard about an answer, and soon it came to him: a man!
When he is a baby, a man crawls on all fours. Then he walks on two legs as
an adult, and finally on three when he is old and needs a cane.

The Sphinx, unable to bear the sound of Oedipus's words, hurled itself off the cliff. Its body broke into pieces bouncing from rock to rock and disappeared in the waves.

SPLASH!

Oedipus walked toward one of the seven gates of Thebes. Its heavy doors swung open, and out poured a joyous crowd. From the ramparts, the Thebans had seen him vanquish the Sphinx.

FINALLY! FREE OF THE SPHINX!

YOU ARE OUR **HERO**!

OPEN ALL THE GATES!

HURRAAAAH!

They led him in triumph to the palace. Their king had died years ago, slain by bandits while traveling. The entire population proclaimed Oedipus king.

OEDIPUS, OUR KING— YOU MUST TAKE QUEEN JOCASTA AS YOUR WIFE.

So, Oedipus married the Queen, not knowing it was his mother, Jocasta. He reigned with her over the kingdom of Boeotia and its capital city, Thebes.

This unnatural union produced two sons, Eteocles* and Polynices,* and two daughters, Antigone* and Ismene.* Twenty years of peace and prosperity passed...

* E·TE·O·CLES [uh-*tee*-oh-kleez] / PO·LY·NI·CES [pahl-ee-*nigh*-seez]
AN·TIG·O·NE [an-*tig*-oh-nee] / IS·ME·NE [ice-*me*-nee]

B ut the gods weren't finished with Oedipus… A new misfortune overcame
Thebes. Black rats overran the city, and an epidemic of the plague* broke
out. Many people died. The angry citizens called upon their king.

*PLAGUE [*plaig*]

Oedipus asked Creon,* his brother-in-law, to go to Delphi to consult the oracle and beg for help from Apollo.

* CRE·ON [*kree*-on]

The Pythia delivered her message.

FIND THE MAN WHO SLEW KING LAIUS AND *PUNISH HIM*. ONLY THEN WILL THE GODS HAVE MERCY AND THE PLAGUE RELENT.

HMMM...

BUT HOW CAN WE FIND THESE BANDITS AFTER MORE THAN TWENTY YEARS?

The Thebans thought they knew who killed Laius: a group of bandits. That was the version given long ago by the guard who escaped when the king was killed.

Oedipus decided to consult the soothsayer Tiresias,* a very old, blind prophet who knew the secrets of all Theban families for six generations. Tiresias came to Thebes but refused to speak of the death of Laius.

TELL ME WHAT I NEED TO KNOW, OLD MAN. MY PEOPLE ARE DYING IN THE STREETS...

DO NOT MAKE ME ANGRY!

Oedipus begged him, but Tiresias remained silent. He threatened him, and the soothsayer became furious.

MAY YOU BE **CURSED**, OEDIPUS! YOU WHO HAD SWORN *NEVER* AGAIN TO GIVE IN TO ANGER!

EVERYTHING YOU WANT TO KNOW IS RIGHT BEFORE *YOU*!

FOR REFUSING TO SEE, YOU WILL BE DEPRIVED OF YOUR *SIGHT*. YOU WILL WANDER THE WORLD, GROPING, TESTING THE GROUND WITH YOUR STICK!

AND EVERYONE, HEARING YOUR NAME, WILL REMEMBER YOUR CRIMES AND AVOID YOU!

* TI·RE·SI·AS [ti-*ree*-see-iss]

Jocasta knew about prophecies not coming true. She told Oedipus that when she was married to Laius, an oracle had foreseen the birth of a son who would kill his father before marrying his mother. Neither one of these disasters had happened. She had indeed had a son, but he had been taken away by a servant who left him to die on Mount Cithaeron. As for Laius, as everyone knew, he had been killed by bandits at the place where three roads meet, not far from Delphi.

At these words, Oedipus's blood froze. This was the first time he had heard this detail concerning the place of the crime. He saw himself as a young man again, at the place where three roads meet, with a bloody sword in his hand.

HOW MANY MEN WERE WITH LAIUS THAT DAY?

FIVE...ALL OF THEM KILLED EXCEPT ONE.

IS HE STILL ALIVE?

YES. HE WAS LAIUS'S MOST LOYAL SERVANT.

TELL ME—IS HE THE ONE WHO CARRIED OFF YOUR FIRST SON TO THE TOP OF MOUNT CITHAERON?

YES...BUT...WHY ARE YOU ASKING ALL THESE QUESTIONS?

Now Jocasta was trembling. Speaking softly but forcefully, Oedipus ordered:
"Send for him right away."

Jocasta obeyed, seized by a terrifying premonition. Oedipus was sixteen years younger than she, and she was sixteen when she gave birth to Laius's son. The murdered king's faithful servant was a very old man who walked with difficulty, as if he were under the weight of a huge burden. "The burden of a secret," thought Oedipus.

I WAS GIVEN A CHILD BY LAIUS. I ABANDONED IT, WITH ITS FEET TIED TOGETHER, AT THE TOP OF MOUNT CITHAERON.
Oedipus then understood why he felt he had already seen the place when, as an adult, he climbed the mountain.
I WAS THAT CHILD. SOMEONE SAVED ME, CARRIED ME AWAY, AND GAVE ME TO THE KING AND QUEEN OF CORINTH.

TWENTY YEARS LATER, IN DELPHI, I KILLED AN OLD MAN AT A PLACE WHERE THREE ROADS MET.
THAT DAY, UNBEKNOWNST TO YOU, YOU SAW ME FOR THE SECOND TIME. WHY DID YOU TELL THIS STORY ABOUT ***BANDITS***?
I WAS ASHAMED THAT ONE MAN ALONE HAD DEFEATED ALL OF US.
YOU SAW ME A THIRD TIME THE DAY OF MY VICTORY OVER THE SPHINX. YOU RECOGNIZED THE MAN WHO HAD KILLED LAIUS, AND THEN THIS VERY MAN MARRIED JOCASTA. YOU UNDERSTOOD THAT THE ORACLE OF DELPHI HAD BEEN FULFILLED.
YOU WERE THE ONLY ONE WHO KNEW THE TRUTH. WHY DID YOU HIDE IT FOR SO MANY YEARS?
I DIDN'T WANT TO CREATE ANY MORE UNHAPPINESS, MY KING.

As he was leaving, the old man passed a servant in tears. She had
come running to tell Oedipus the terrible news.

Laius and Jocasta, cursed by the gods! And he, Oedipus, cursed three times!
He had killed his father, married his mother, and also broken his adoptive parents'
hearts by leaving them… All of this as a result of an oracle pronounced even before
he was born. Innocent victim at the start of his life, infant abandoned to the lions
and the vultures—what had he done to deserve his fate, he wondered. He was only
the victim of a cruel game invented by the gods of Mount Olympus.

The soothsayer Tiresias then stood before him,
as if he had appeared from nowhere.

DO NOT ACCUSE THE GODS, OEDIPUS!
YOU LET YOUR ANGER LOOSE ON A MAN
OLDER THAN YOU. YOU TOOK ANOTHER'S
LIFE WITH IMPUNITY. IT IS ONLY JUST
THAT TODAY ALL THE BLOOD YOU SHED IS
BEING POURED UPON YOU.

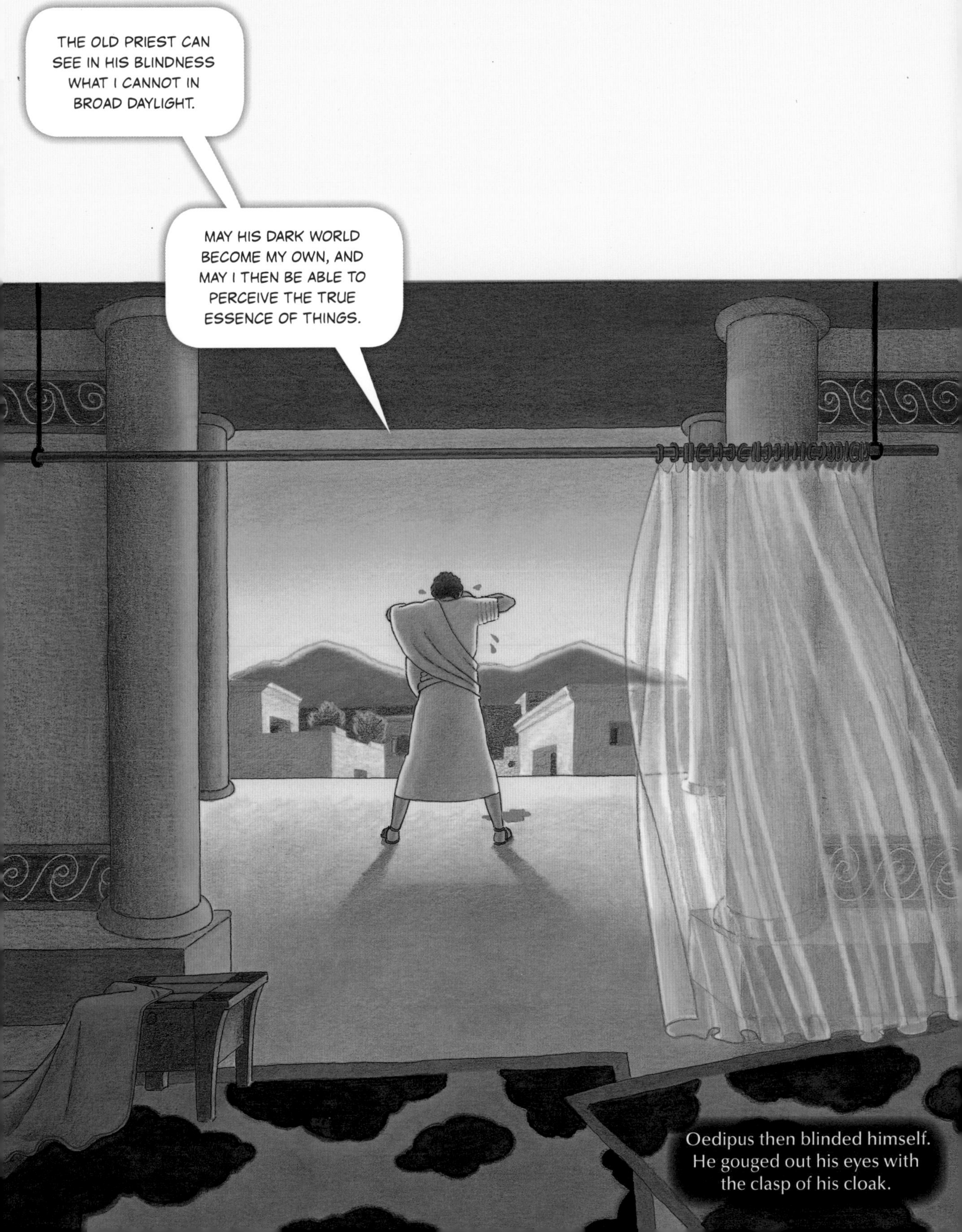
THE OLD PRIEST CAN SEE IN HIS BLINDNESS WHAT I CANNOT IN BROAD DAYLIGHT.
MAY HIS DARK WORLD BECOME MY OWN, AND MAY I THEN BE ABLE TO PERCEIVE THE TRUE ESSENCE OF THINGS.
Oedipus then blinded himself. He gouged out his eyes with the clasp of his cloak.

The rats that had brought the plague left Thebes, but no one knew that the epidemic was over. The people shut themselves away, and Oedipus walked through deserted streets with his daughter Antigone.

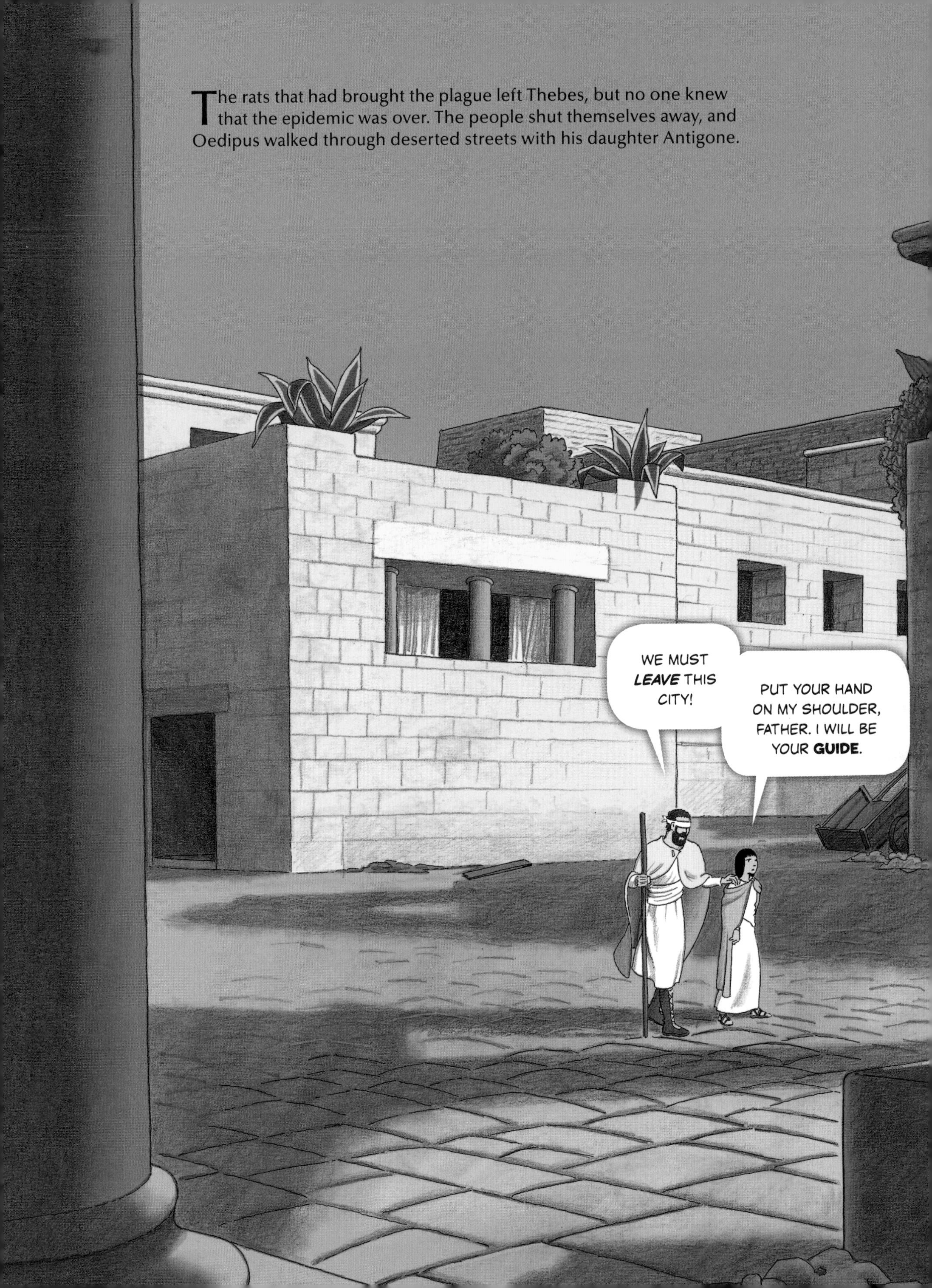

WE MUST *LEAVE* THIS CITY!
PUT YOUR HAND ON MY SHOULDER, FATHER. I WILL BE YOUR **GUIDE**.

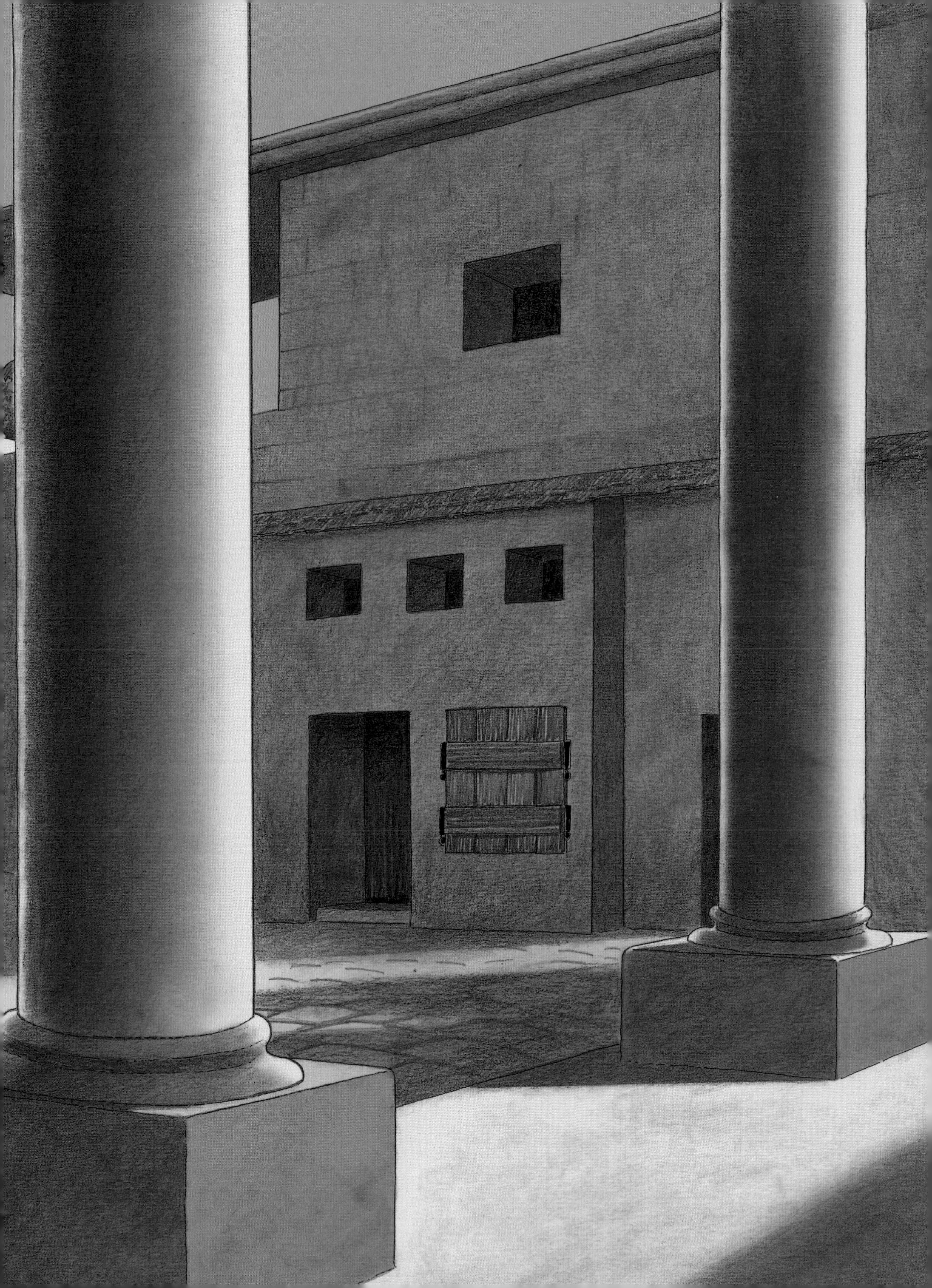

Oedipus and Antigone crossed through many lands. The young girl was loving and attentive. Their wandering, which little by little became known to everyone, caused people to honor them.

One day, he came to Theseus,* the founder, king, and hero of Ancient Athens, and asked for permission to stay there until his death. After hearing his story, Theseus felt pity for Oedipus and granted him his wish. And so Oedipus, a man with a tragic life, ended it in peace.

GRANDPA, THAT'S A HORRIBLE STORY!

YES, BUT IT WAS WAY MORE THAN TRAGIC!

I WARNED YOU THAT IT WAS TRAGIC.

AND THE STORY OF ANTIGONE, AFTERWARD... IS IT MORE FUN THAN HER FATHER'S?

YOU'VE GOT TO BE KIDDING ME!

NO, I BELIEVE IT'S EVEN WORSE!

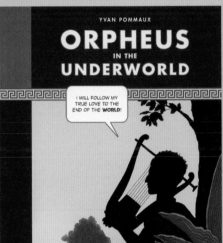

Comics and Graphics

TOON Graphics are comics and visual narratives that bring the text to life in a way that captures young readers' imaginations and makes them want to read on—and read more. When the authors are also artists, they can convey their creative vision with pictures as well as words. They can enhance the overarching theme and present important details that are absorbed by the reader along with the text. Young readers also develop their aesthetic sense when they experience the relationship of text to picture in all its communicative power.

Reading TOON Graphics is a pleasure for all. Beginners and seasoned readers alike will sharpen both their literal and inferential reading skills.

Let the pictures tell the story

The very economy of comic books necessitates the use of a reader's imaginative powers. In comics, the images often imply rather than tell outright. Readers must learn to make connections between events to complete the narrative, helping them build their ability to visualize and to make "mental maps."

A comic book also gives readers a great deal of visual context that can be used to investigate the thinking behind the characters' choices.

Pay attention to the artist's choices

Look carefully at the artwork: it offers a subtext that at first is sensed only on a subliminal level by the reader and encourages rereading. It creates a sense of continuity for the action, and it can tell you about the art, architecture, and clothing of a specific time period. It may present the atmosphere, landscape, and flora and fauna of another time or of another part of the world. TOON Graphics can also present multiple points of view and simultaneous events in a manner not permitted by linear written narration. Facial expressions and body language reveal subtle aspects of characters' personalities beyond what can be expressed by words.

Read and reread!

Readers can compare comic book artists' styles and evaluate how different authors get their point across in different ways. In investigating the author's choices, a young reader begins to gain a sense of how all literary and art forms can be used to convey the author's central ideas. The world of TOON Graphics and of comic book art is rich and varied. Making meaning out of reading with the aid of visuals may be the best way to become a lifelong reader, one who knows how to read for pleasure and for information—a reader who *loves* to read.

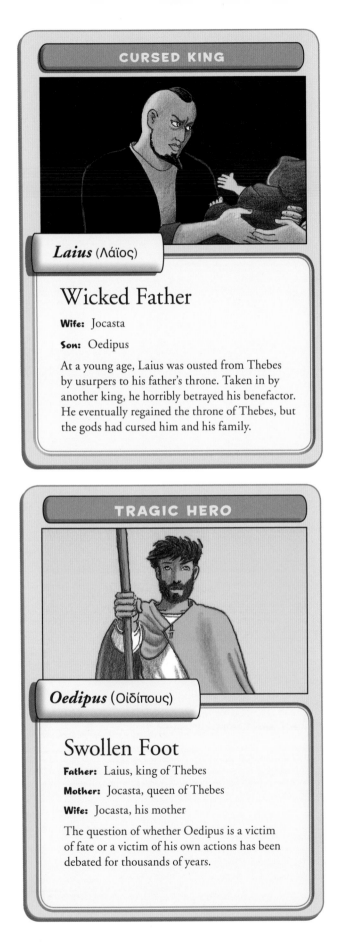

Laius (Λάϊος)

Wicked Father

Wife: Jocasta

Son: Oedipus

At a young age, Laius was ousted from Thebes by usurpers to his father's throne. Taken in by another king, he horribly betrayed his benefactor. He eventually regained the throne of Thebes, but the gods had cursed him and his family.

Jocasta (Ἰοκάστη)

Also known as **Epicaste** (in Homer)

Husbands: Laius and her son, Oedipus

Brother: Creon

Child with Laius: Oedipus

Children with Oedipus: Two boys, Polynices and Eteocles, and two girls, Ismene and Antigone. After Oedipus blinded himself and left Thebes, Polynices and Eteocles fought for the throne and killed each other.

Oedipus (Οἰδίπους)

Swollen Foot

Father: Laius, king of Thebes

Mother: Jocasta, queen of Thebes

Wife: Jocasta, his mother

The question of whether Oedipus is a victim of fate or a victim of his own actions has been debated for thousands of years.

Antigone (Ἀντιγόνη)

Against Ancestors

Parents: Oedipus, her father and brother, and Jocasta, her mother and grandmother

Siblings: Ismene, Polynices, Eteocles, and Oedipus, her father

Antigone guided her blind father in his old age. Later she became a symbol of rebellion against the state when she defied her uncle, King Creon.

POWERFUL PRIESTESS

The Pythia (Πυθία)

Oracle of Delphi

Power: predicting the future

The Pythia went into a trance to deliver prophecies. Her grunts and cries were then interpreted by priests. It is now thought that the trances may have been caused by fumes seeping up from the rocks where she sat or by the plants burned during the ceremonies.

MYTHICAL CREATURE

The Sphinx (Σφίγξ)

Strangler (from "sphingo": to strangle)

In Greek tradition, the Sphinx is a monster with the head of a woman, the wings of a griffin, and the body of a lion. In the earlier Egyptian myths, its head is that of a man.

GOD OF LIGHT AND SUN

Apollo (Ἀπόλλων)

Synonymous with # Manly Beauty

Parents: Zeus, king of the gods, and the Titaness Leto

Children: Asclepius (the god of Healing), the legendary musician Orpheus, and the heroes Troilus and Aristaeus

Powers: Apollo was the god of prophecy, medicine, music, art, poetry, law and wisdom. His tree was the laurel.

BLIND SEER

Tiresias (Τειρεσίας)

Sign, portent

Powers: predicting the future, understanding birds

Parents: Everes, a shepherd, and Chariclo, a nymph

Tiresias spent seven years as a woman–and even raised a family–before being a man again. Hera cursed him with blindness, but Zeus granted him a very long life and the power to see the future.

INDEX

ANTIGONE—One of Oedipus's two daughters by Jocasta–Antigone was therefore both the daughter and the sister of her father, a disturbing situation. Despite this most difficult state of affairs, she was a model of devotion, both fraternal and filial. She served first as the blind Oedipus's guide but later was put to death for wanting a proper burial for her brother, Polynices (p. 27, 40, 42).

APOLLO—Son of Zeus, king of the gods. Apollo was the god of light (he controlled the sun), medicine (assisted by his son Asclepius), and the arts (in his role as supervisor of the Muses). He was also very good-looking and was considered the model of manly beauty. Even today, we still call a handsome man an Apollo (p. 9-10, 29).

BOEOTIA—A region in the center of Ancient Greece, next to Phocis. The ancient Greeks thought that its misty climate affected the intelligence of its inhabitants, making them them slow-witted (p. 2, 20, 27).

CITHAERON—A mountain overlooking the sea, not far from Thebes, in Boeotia. Its summit was supposed to have been particularly unwelcoming. In theory, if one abandoned a newborn there with its legs tied together, it would die from cold or hunger or be devoured by wild beasts. Oedipus survived because a shepherd, Phorbas, found him (p. 2, 11, 21, 32, 33-35).

CORINTH—Port city of Greece, at the east end of the Gulf of Corinth (p. 2, 11, 12-13, 18, 35).

CREON—Legendary king of Thebes, who inherited the throne after his two nephews, Polynices and Eteocles (see later), killed each other trying to seize power. An inflexible man, he had their sister Antigone put to death for daring to throw a handful of earth on Polynices's body after he had forbidden his burial. This confrontation of uncle and niece, subject of many plays and other literary works, is still a model for the conflict between the power of the state and an individual's moral judgment (p. 29).

DELPHI—City of Ancient Greece, in Phocis, where the most famous temple of Apollo stood (p. 2, 9, 13, 29, 32, 36).

ETEOCLES—One of Jocasta and Oedipus's children. After Oedipus stepped down from his throne, Eteocles and his brother Polynices took turns reigning over Thebes. But in a struggle for a permanent hold on the throne, they killed each other. Their uncle Creon, seeing the throne empty, assumed power, but having taken Eteocles's side, he forbade the burial of Polynices. It was against this decree that their sister Antigone protested, an act of disobedience that would cost her her life (p. 27).

ISMENE—Polynices and Eteocles's other sister, also the daughter of Oedipus and Jocasta. She did not have Antigone's rebellious temperament. Ismene obeyed the decree of her uncle Creon, the new king of Thebes, who forbade the burial of Polynices (p. 27).

JOCASTA—Sister of Creon, she at first married Laius, king of Thebes. They had a son, the future Oedipus, and ordered that he be abandoned on the top of Mount Cithaeron. But this attempt at infanticide failed, and the Pythia's prediction came true: Oedipus killed Laius without meaning to and married Jocasta without knowing who she was (p. 9, 11, 26-27, 32-34, 36-37).

LAIUS—Legendary king of Thebes. He was the third in descent from Cadmus, who founded the city of Thebes at Apollo's urging. Laius married his distant cousin, Jocasta (p. 9-11, 30, 32, 33-37).

MOUNT OLYMPUS— The inaccessible place above the clouds where the gods dwelled, amusing themselves in their leisure time by eating ambrosia, drinking nectar, and watching the spectacle below of humans dealing with their troubles (p. 37).

MEROPE—Wife of Polybus, king of Corinth. Unable to have children, the king and queen were overjoyed to adopt the baby brought to them by Phorbas (see below). They named him Oedipus ("swollen feet"), a result of his ankles being tied together before he was abandoned on Mount Cithaeron (p. 12, 18, 35).

OEDIPUS—Hero of this book. He represents the idea that one cannot escape his or her fate. The crimes he committed, killing his father and marrying his mother, were unintentional. As soon as he discovered them, he was horrified and overcome with despair (p. 8, 12-21, 24-40, 42).

ORACLE—The answer given by the gods to a question asked by humans, the person giving the answer, and the name of the sanctuary where this took place. Thus, the Temple of Delphi, where the oracle Pythia pronounced Apollo's oracles, was itself an oracle (p. 10, 13-15, 29, 32, 36-37).

PHOCIS—A mountainous region next to Boeotia, home of the Temple of Apollo at Delphi. Pilgrims who wanted to learn about their future or were worried about their health came to the Temple to hear the god's predictions (p. 2).